D0131764

Swim the Silver Sea, Joshie Otter

by Nancy White Carlstrom

illustrated by Ken Kuroi

PAPERSTAR

The Putnam & Grosset Group

Printed on recycled paper

Text copyright © 1993 by Nancy White Carlstrom
Illustrations copyright © 1993 by Ken Kuroi
All rights reserved. This book, or parts thereof, may not be reproduced
in any form without permission in writing from the publisher.
A PaperStar Book, published in 1997 by The Putnam & Grosset Group,
200 Madison Avenue, New York, NY 10016. PaperStar Books and
the PaperStar logo are trademarks of The Putnam Berkley Group, Inc.
Originally published in 1993 by Philomel Books.
Published simultaneously in Canada.
Printed in the United States of America.

Library of Congress Cataloging-in-Publication Data
Carlstrom, Nancy White.
Swim the silver sea, Joshie Otter/by Nancy White Carlstrom;
illustrated by Ken Kuroi. p. cm.
Summary: Because none of the other animals will play with him,
Joshie the sea otter swims too far out to sea, but he is called
back by a song sung in the strong safe voice of his mother.
[1. Sea otter—Fiction. 2. Otters—Fiction.] I. Kuroi, Ken,
1947– ill. II. Title.
PZ7.C21684Sw 1993 [E]—dc20 91-26168 CIP AC
ISBN 0-698-11447-7
10 9 8 7

For Joshua White Carlstrom,
the real Joshie Otter,
with love—NWC

To my father—KK

Joshua Otter wanted to play.
"Oh no, not today," said his mama.

She called, "Stop right now."
But he swam far away
to the great gray rocks
of the seal baby pups.
But those pups were asleep
and they didn't hear him
and they wouldn't wake up.

So he swam to the brown
walrus calves on the sand.
And he asked them politely
please once,
then please twice.
But they couldn't come down
and they wouldn't come play.

So Joshua Otter
swam farther away
to the sky-climbing cliffs
of the puffins.
But the puffins were resting
not wanting to swim
not noticing him
thinking only
of nesting in crevices.

The kittiwakes too
all had something to do
as they stood red-legged
squawking on perches.

While the murres dove down deep
fishing to eat,
and the arctic fox
wily stalked, watching.

Poor Joshua Otter
who wanted to play
swam out of day into night.
And was lost
in the very dark
scary dark sea.
Joshua Otter
afraid and alone
Joshua Otter
was farther from home
than ever before
in his life.

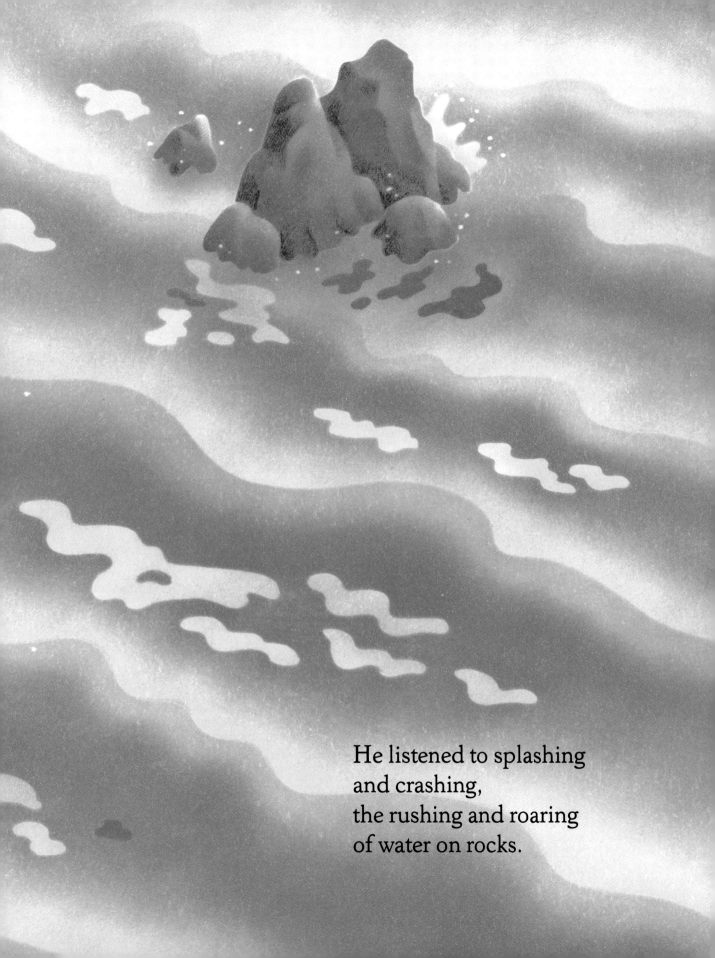

He listened to splashing
and crashing,
the rushing and roaring
of water on rocks.

Then over the waves
came the words of a song
calling and calling
and calling his name.
The strong safe voice of his mama.

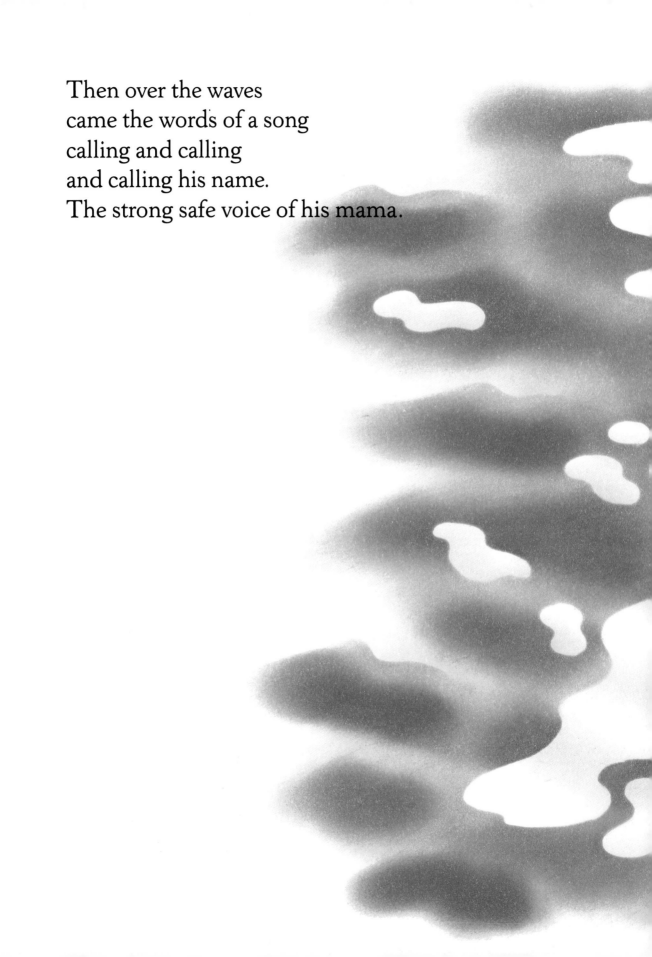

Swim the silver sea, Joshie Otter
Swim on home to me, Joshie Otter
While night stirs above
Come to me, my love
And swim the silver sea, my Joshie Otter.

Dive the silver sea, Joshie Otter
Dive on home to me, Joshie Otter
When the moon comes up
Brave the waves, my pup
And dive the silver sea, my Joshie Otter.

He swam past the fox
still looking for eggs,

the black and white murres
and the birds with red legs.

He swam past the puffins on cliffs.

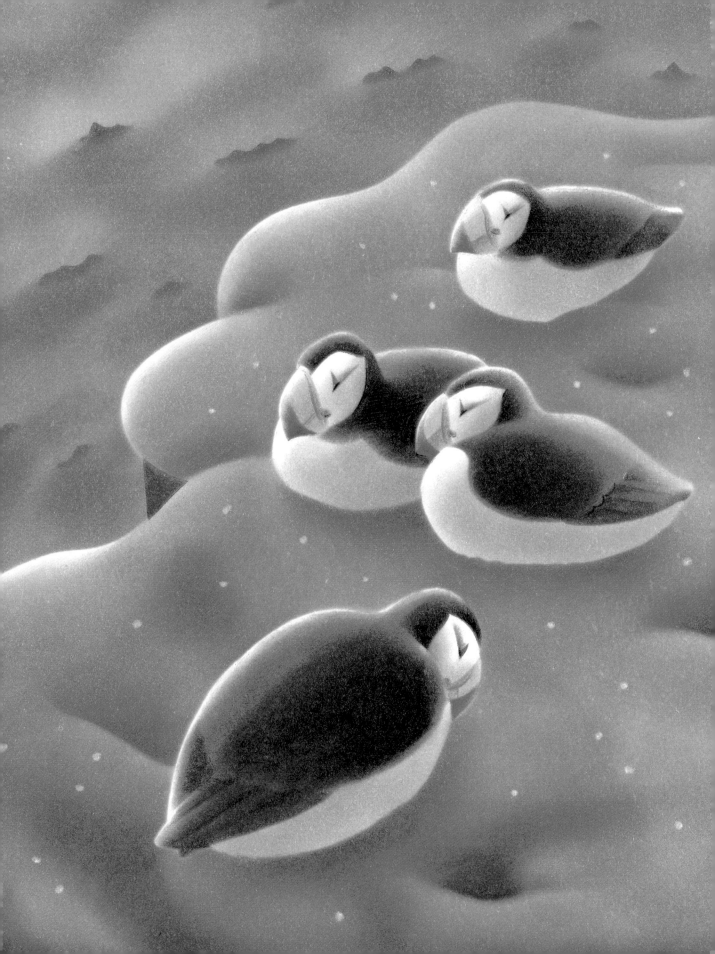

He swam past the brown
walrus calves on the sand

and the seal baby pups
at the great gray rocks.

He followed that song
over waves in the night
on the billowy deep
through the silver moonlight.
Those words pulled him home.

And mama was waiting
to put him to bed.
Joshua Otter slept all through the night.
He slept and he dreamt
then they greeted the day.

Joshie and Mama,
two otters at play.

Swim the Silver Sea, Joshie Otter

Words and music—N. W. Carlstrom,
arranged by Leslie Salisbury

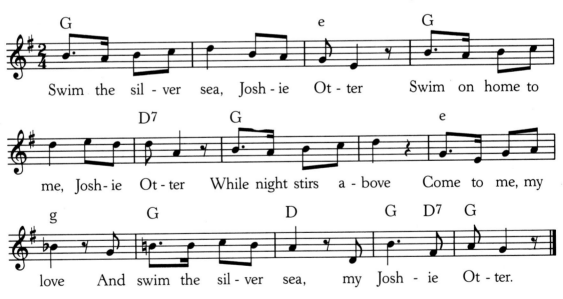

Swim the sil-ver sea, Josh-ie Ot-ter Swim on home to me, Josh-ie Ot-ter While night stirs a-bove Come to me, my love And swim the sil-ver sea, my Josh-ie Ot-ter.

Dive the silver sea, Joshie Otter
Dive on home to me, Joshie Otter
When the moon comes up
Brave the waves, my pup
And dive the silver sea, my Joshie Otter.

Float the silver sea, Joshie Otter
Float on home to me, Joshie Otter
As stars fill the sky
You'll come shining by
And float the silver sea, my Joshie Otter.